Dear Parent:

Congratulations! Your child is taking the first steps on an exciting journey. The destination? Independent reading!

STEP INTO READING® will help your child get there. The program offers books at five levels that accompany children from their first attempts at reading to reading success. Each step includes fun stories, fiction and nonfiction, and colorful art. There are also Step into Reading Sticker Books, Step into Reading Math Readers, and Step into Reading Phonics Readers— a complete literacy program with something to interest every child.

Learning to Read, Step by Step!

Ready to Read   Preschool–Kindergarten
• big type and easy words • rhyme and rhythm • picture clues
For children who know the alphabet and are eager to begin reading.

Reading with Help   Preschool–Grade 1
• basic vocabulary • short sentences • simple stories
For children who recognize familiar words and sound out new words with help.

Reading on Your Own   Grades 1–3
• engaging characters • easy-to-follow plots • popular topics
For children who are ready to read on their own.

Reading Paragraphs   Grades 2–3
• challenging vocabulary • short paragraphs • exciting stories
For newly independent readers who read simple sentences with confidence.

Ready for Chapters   Grades 2–4
• chapters • longer paragraphs • full-color art
For children who want to take the plunge into chapter books but still like colorful pictures.

STEP INTO READING® is designed to give every child a successful reading experience. The grade levels are only guides. Children can progress through the steps at their own speed, developing confidence in their reading, no matter what their grade.

Remember, a lifetime love of reading starts with a single step!

To Paul, who has the biggest heart
—J. W.

Copyright © 2002 Disney Enterprises, Inc. Based on the "Winnie the Pooh" works by
A. A. Milne and E. H. Shepard. All rights reserved under International and Pan-American
Copyright Conventions. Published in the United States by Random House Children's Books,
a division of Random House, Inc., New York, and simultaneously in Canada by Random House
of Canada Limited, Toronto.

www.stepintoreading.com

Educators and librarians, for a variety of teaching tools, visit us at
www.randomhouse.com/teachers

Library of Congress Cataloging-in-Publication Data
Weinberg, Jennifer, 1970–.
Piglet feels small / by Jennifer Liberts Weinberg ; illustrated by Josie Yee.
   p.   cm. — (Step into reading. A step 1 book)
SUMMARY: Piglet feels sad because he's too small to climb trees or fly kites until his friends
remind him of the many things he can do.
ISBN 0-7364-1226-3 (trade) — ISBN 0-7364-8003-X (lib. bdg.)
[1. Size—Fiction.   2. Pigs—Fiction.   3. Toys—Fiction.   4. Stories in rhyme.]
I. Yee, Josie, ill.   II. Title.   III. Step into reading. Step 1 book.
PZ8.3.W4213 Pi 2003 [E]—dc21   2002012980

Printed in the United States of America 10 9 8

STEP INTO READING, RANDOM HOUSE, and the Random House colophon are registered trademarks
of Random House, Inc.

DISNEY
Winnie the Pooh

Piglet Feels Small

By Jennifer Liberts Weinberg

Illustrated by Josie Yee

Random House 🏠 New York

Pooh can climb a tree!

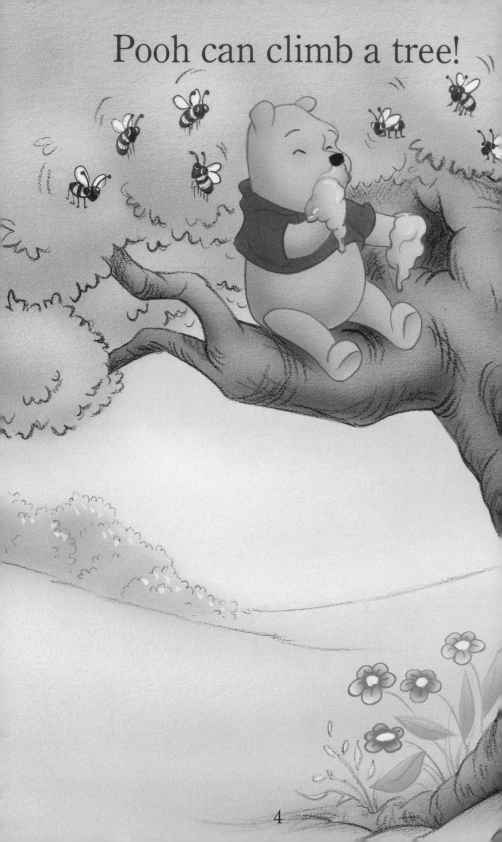

Piglet is too small
to climb a tree.

Tigger can bounce high.

Piglet is too small
to bounce high.

Christopher Robin
can fly a kite.

Oh, dear!

Piglet is too small

to fly a kite.

"I am too small
to do anything at all!"
says Piglet.

Pooh tells his sad friend,
"But look at all
that you <u>can</u> do."

"You can pick berries,"
says Pooh.

"You can plant seeds,"
says Pooh.

Piglet is a big help
to Rabbit.

"Yes!" says Piglet.
"And I can share
with you and Eeyore."

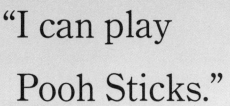

"I can play

Pooh Sticks."

"And I can count!"

Piglet shouts.

One, two, three!

"I can hum a sunny tune
with you . . .

. . . and play
follow-the-leader, too!"

When someone is sad,

being small is not bad.

Piglet can give big hugs,

and make a friend smile!

Piglet always goes
the extra mile.

Piglet is small,

that is true . . .

... but he can do
lots of things,
just like you!